# The Little Germ
# that Travelled the World

A story for children about social distancing

Written and Illustrated by

By Imelda Bell

This story is dedicated to all the key workers
to thank them for all they are doing to help others.

Printed in the United Kingdom
First Printing 2020
ISBN 9798646116803

www.photographybyImelda.co.uk

There once was a little germ called Coronavirus or COVID-19,

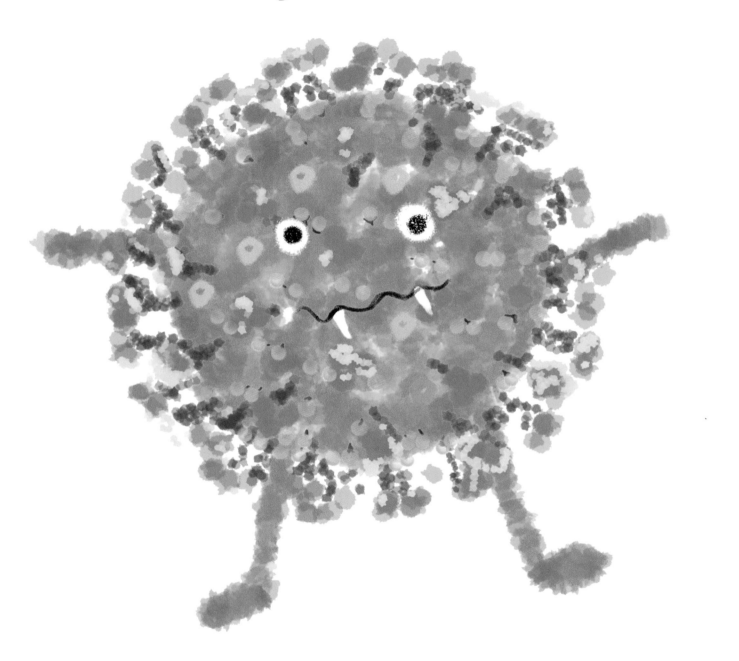

he wanted to travel, but had to do it unseen,

so he packed a bag, to hitch a ride

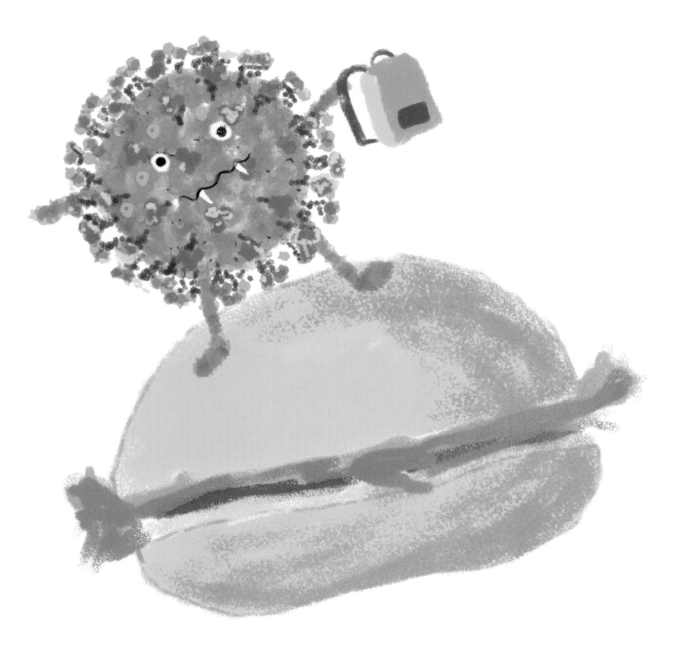

and when a man  along came, he crept inside.

Inside the man, one germ became two

and soon there were more germs, not just a few!

The germs had a party and couldn't stay still

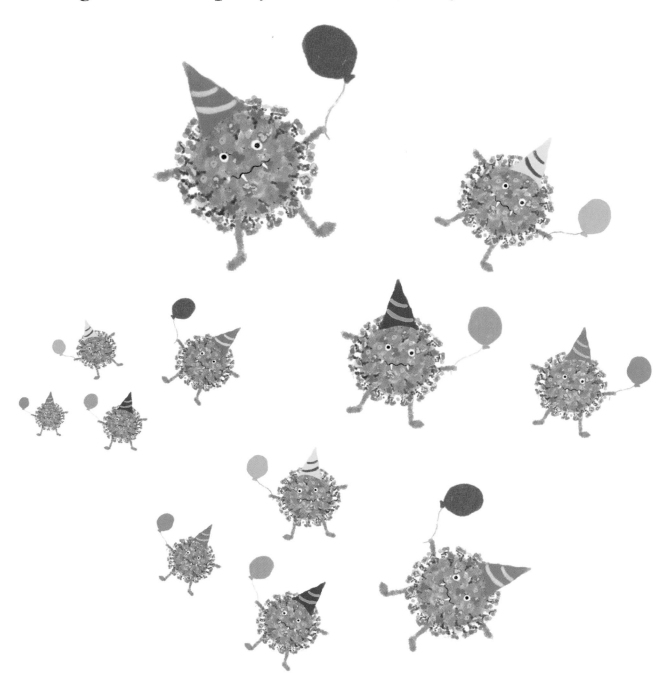

and soon the man started to feel a little bit ill.

The man coughed and made the germs fly

and they landed on a passer by.

And one passer by soon became two,

more people got ill, not just a few.

And so the germ called COVID-19

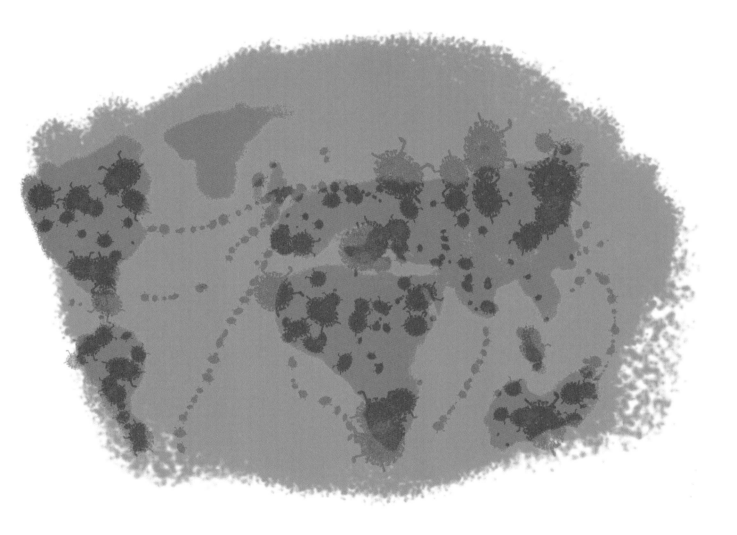

travelled the world and became very mean.

Soon he was making lots of us sick

but people were smarter and came up with a trick

The germs can travel, but not more than **2** metres,

so if we stay apart, they won't learn to beat us.

To make sure we stuck to this rule,

children had to learn at home, not in school.

We had to stay indoors and off the street,

no visiting friends or going out to eat.

Just once a day, we went out for a walk or run,

we only bought food when we needed some.

Doctors and nurses worked day and night,

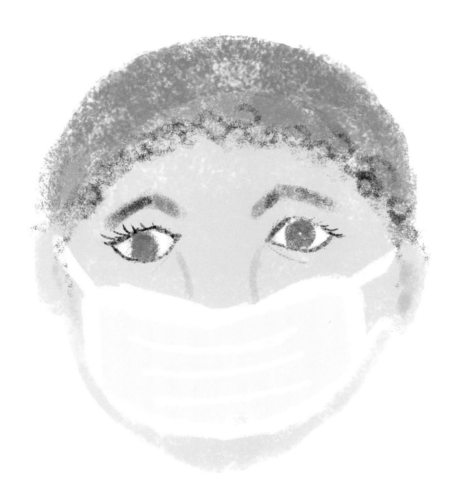

but they asked us all to help in this fight.

Key workers had to work hard to help others

and lots of them were fathers and mothers

It was a difficult time, but we had to do our bit

to fight the virus and not quit.

On a Thursday evening at eight on the dot,

we clapped and cheered or banged on a pot

for postman, drivers & carers and people working in shops,

for health workers and cleaners, as well as the cops,

for the ordinary people, who without knowing,

became the heroes who kept the country going.

Rainbows in windows spread hope and belief

that soon we would get through our grief.

One thing the germs do not like is soap,

so to COVID-19, hand washing was no joke.

Washing your hands throughout the day

helps to keep the Coronavirus away.

And when people started to stay inside

COVID-19 had nowhere to hide.

So Coronavirus had nowhere to go

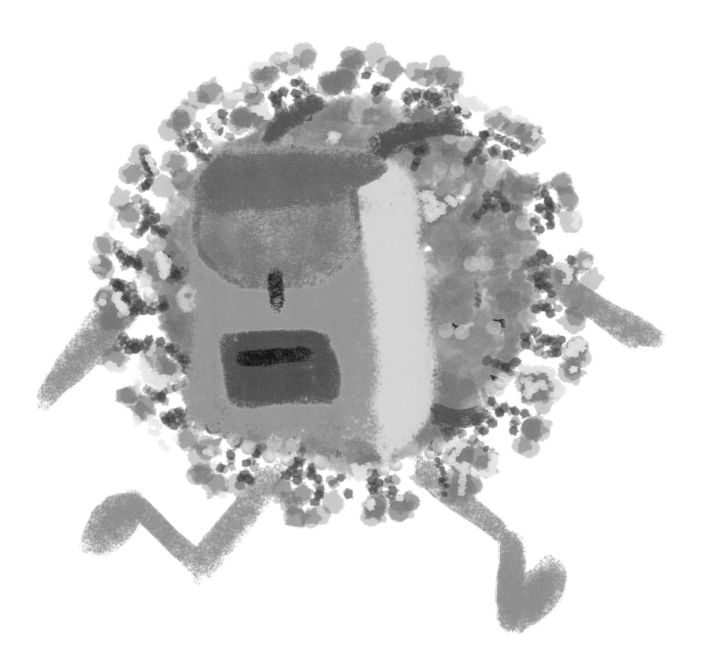

and the infection soon began to slow.

Although life may seem hard and you may be scared

just look for rainbows and remember how people cared.

This is book is my "rainbow in the window"
and my gift to children.


You can hear me reading the story on you tube.

https://youtu.be/xuyBKubaUAg

If you are able to make a donation
to charity, it would be very much appreciated.

I have chosen the following 2 charities to support
NHS Charities Together
https://www.nhscharitiestogether.co.uk
and
Care International's Covid -19 Emergency Appeal
https://www.careinternational.org.uk/emergencies/covid-19-emergency

or see the just giving links in my
you tube video description to donate.

Thank you so much.
Every penny is appreciated.

Printed in Poland
by Amazon Fulfillment
Poland Sp. z o.o., Wrocław

63942499R00019